Mount Rushmore

Risa Brown

FITZGERALD
BOOKS

Bethany, Missouri

Photo Credits:
Cover © Photodisc, National Park Service; Title Page, Pages 8, 15 © Photodisc; Pages 4, 5 © John Woodworth;
Pages 7, 9, 12, 14 © Library of Congress; Pages 10, 13, 16, 17, 18, 19, 20, 21 © National Park Service;
Page 22 © Arian Kulp

Cataloging-in-Publication Data

Brown, Risa W.
    Mount Rushmore / Risa Brown. — 1st ed.
    p. cm. — (National places)

    Includes bibliographical references and index.
    Summary: Text and photographs introduce Mount Rushmore,
the brave efforts of all who helped to create it, and the sculptor Gutzon Borglum.
    ISBN-13: 978-1-4242-1369-6 (lib. bdg. : alk. paper)
    ISBN-10: 1-4242-1369-X (lib. bdg. : alk. paper)
    ISBN-13: 978-1-4242-1459-4 (pbk. : alk. paper)
    ISBN-10: 1-4242-1459-9 (pbk. : alk. paper)

    1. Mount Rushmore National Memorial (S.D.)—Juvenile literature.
[1. Mount Rushmore National Memorial (S.D.). 2. National monuments.
3. Borglum, Gutzon, 1867-1941. 4. Monuments.] I. Brown, Risa W.
II. Title. III. Series.
    F657.R8B76 2007
    978.3'93—dc22

First edition
© 2007 Fitzgerald Books
802 N. 41st Street, P.O. Box 505
Bethany, MO 64424, U.S.A.
Printed in China
Library of Congress Control Number: 2006940991

Table of Contents

George Washington

Thomas Jefferson

Theodore Roosevelt

4

World's Largest Statue

The largest faces ever carved can be seen at Mt. Rushmore. The faces **honor** four American heroes: George Washington, Thomas Jefferson, Theodore Roosevelt, and Abraham Lincoln.

Abraham Lincoln

5

Why These Presidents?

Each of these presidents helped America become great. Washington is known as the "Father of Our Country," and Jefferson helped the country grow.

Washington

Lincoln kept the country together and freed the slaves during the **Civil War**. Roosevelt helped the country become wealthy.

Lincoln

Roosevelt

9

South Dakota

In 1925, a group in South Dakota wanted to build a large **monument** to bring visitors to the state. The Black Hills and Mt. Rushmore looked like the perfect spot.

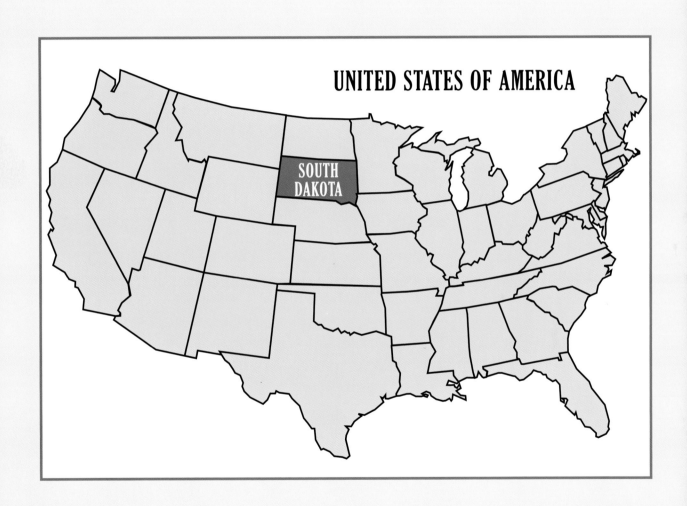

UNITED STATES OF AMERICA

SOUTH
DAKOTA

The Artist

Gutzon Borglum was a **sculptor**. He figured out a way to carve his idea into the mountain.

How Borglum Did It

Borglum made **models** first. Then he invented a machine that showed workers where to carve on the mountain.

Drillers

Large amounts of stone were blasted away. Workers called drillers used **jackhammers** to make holes for the **dynamite**.

Stonecutters

To make the faces appear, workers called stonecutters carved, shaping the rocks with hammers and **chisels**.

19

Dangerous Work

The crew learned to do its work, hanging from **cables**. One by one the faces were finished. The work ended in 1941.

Spirit of America

Mt. Rushmore and its sculpture honors the spirit of America.

Glossary

cable (KAY buhl) — thick, strong ropes

chisel (CHIZ uhl) — a tool to cut away pieces of rock

Civil War (SIV il WOR) — a war in the United States in which the northern states fought against the southern states

dynamite (DYE nuh mite) — an explosive used to blast away bigger pieces of rock

honor (ON ur) — to show respect by doing something special

jackhammer (JAK ham ur) — a drilling tool

monument (MON yuh muhnt) — a special building or statue to help us remember a person or an event

model (MOD uhl) — a small version of a bigger thing

sculptor (SKUHLP tur) — an artist who makes statues

Index

FURTHER READING

Ashley, Susan. *Mount Rushmore*. Weekly Reader, 2006.
Rau, Dana Meachen. *Mount Rushmore*. Compass Point, 2002.
Schaefer, Lola. *Mount Rushmore*. Heinemann, 2002.

WEBSITES TO VISIT

Because Internet links change so often, Fitzgerald Books has developed an online list of websites related to the subject of this book. This site is updated regularly. Please use this link to access the list: www.fitzgeraldbookslinks.com/np/mr

ABOUT THE AUTHOR

Risa Brown was a librarian for twenty years before becoming a full-time writer. Now living in Dallas, she grew up in Midland, Texas, President George W. Bush's hometown.